Marmon
Wasp
(1911)

Bugatti
Type 35
(1924)

Miller 91
(1920s)

Alfa Romeo P3
(1932)

Mercedes-Benz
W154
(1938)

BMW 328
(1940)

Jaguar
C Type
(1951)

Mercedes-Benz
300SL
(1952)

McLaren M23
(1976)

Porsche 956
(1982)

Chevrolet
Monte Carlo
(1995)

Ferrari
F1–2001
(2001)

# THE RACECAR ALPHABET

## A Note On One Hundred Years of Racecars

*The racecar came clattering into the twentieth century as simple as could be—an engine, a chassis, and wheels. At first drivers drove with mechanics at their sides, over roads of rock and gravel, bouncing and shaking every inch of the way.*

*Neither roads nor cars stayed simple for long.*

*Soon drivers were racing on oval courses that were paved with bricks or boards. Racers sped through the old city of Monte Carlo, down narrow streets and around hairpin curves. Road races followed long loops through the countryside. Endurance races kept drivers driving through light and dark, from one afternoon to the next.*

*Until the late 1960s the color of a car often (but not always) told what country the car came from: green cars were British, blue cars were French, gray cars were German, red cars were Italian, and blue-and-white cars were from the United States. Then companies began paying to place their own colors and advertisements on cars. American stock cars became bright jumbles of color, rolling billboards.*

*Different kinds of cars were built for different kinds of races. The machines became sturdier, faster, and more streamlined. They changed so much that a modern Formula 1 racecar hardly seems related to a simple racecar from one hundred years ago. With its airfoils and sleek looks the twenty-first-century machine resembles a jet fighter as much as it does a racecar. But the racecars of each time remain wonderful mechanical sculptures, sculptures on wheels, embodying the appeal and promise of speed.* —B. F.

For Lauren Greenfield

# THE RACECAR
## ALPHABET

*by* BRIAN FLOCA

A Richard Jackson Book • Atheneum Books for Young Readers
New York   London   Toronto   Sydney   Singapore

Atheneum Books for Young Readers
An imprint of Simon & Schuster
Children's Publishing Division
1230 Avenue of the Americas
New York, New York 10020
The text of this book is set in New Century Schoolbook.
The illustrations are rendered in watercolor.
Manufactured in China

7 8 9 10

Library of Congress Cataloging-in-Publication Data
Floca, Brian.
The racecar alphabet / Brian Floca.
p.    cm.
"A Richard Jackson book."
Summary: An exciting day at the races highlights
the letters of the alphabet as a variety of automobiles
burn fuel speeding through the curves of the track.
ISBN-13: 978-0-689-85091-2 (ISBN-10: 0-689-85091-3)
[1. Automobile racing—Fiction. 2. Automobiles,
Racing—Fiction. 3. Alphabet.] I. Title.
PZ7 .F6579 Rac 2003
[E]—dc21       2002002198

Automobiles—
machines on wheels.

Belts turning,
fuel burning,
the buzz and bark of engines.
The flap of a flag—
a race begins!

Curves
across the course
cause cars
to careen
and to crowd
and come close
to colliding.

Drivers
daring,
dodge the danger.

Eyes in the audience,
each open and eager,
expecting excitement
(enduring exhaust).

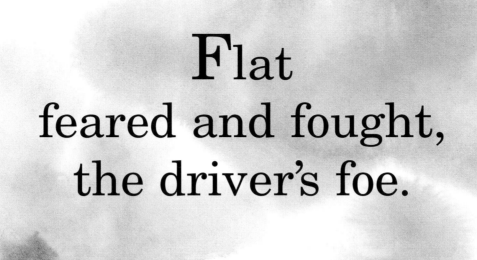

**F**lat
feared and fought,
the driver's foe.

Goggles
guarding sight.

Helmets
holding heads.

Instruments indicating speed.

Jarring,

jerk,

jolt,
and jounce.

Kaput—
a car that has crashed
that no key can start.

Leader
logging laps.

Motor,
mighty motor,
maker of motion—
roars like a monster,
minded and mended
by many mechanics.

Numbers
on noses
needed for knowing
who's now in the lead.

Oval
(over and over).

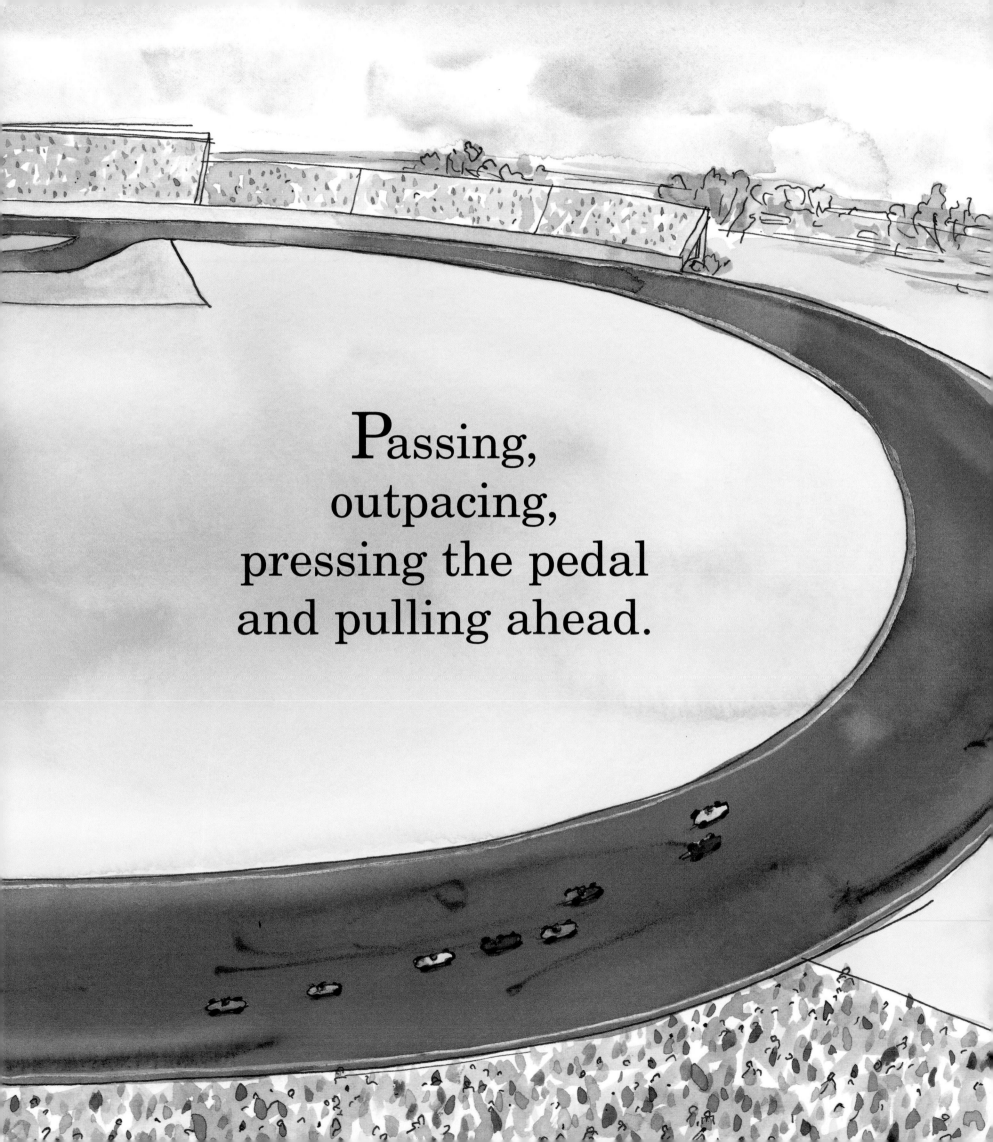

Passing,
outpacing,
pressing the pedal
and pulling ahead.

Quick,
without question.
Quiet?
Not quite.

Racing,
  rapid riding,
    rushing, roaring, risking.

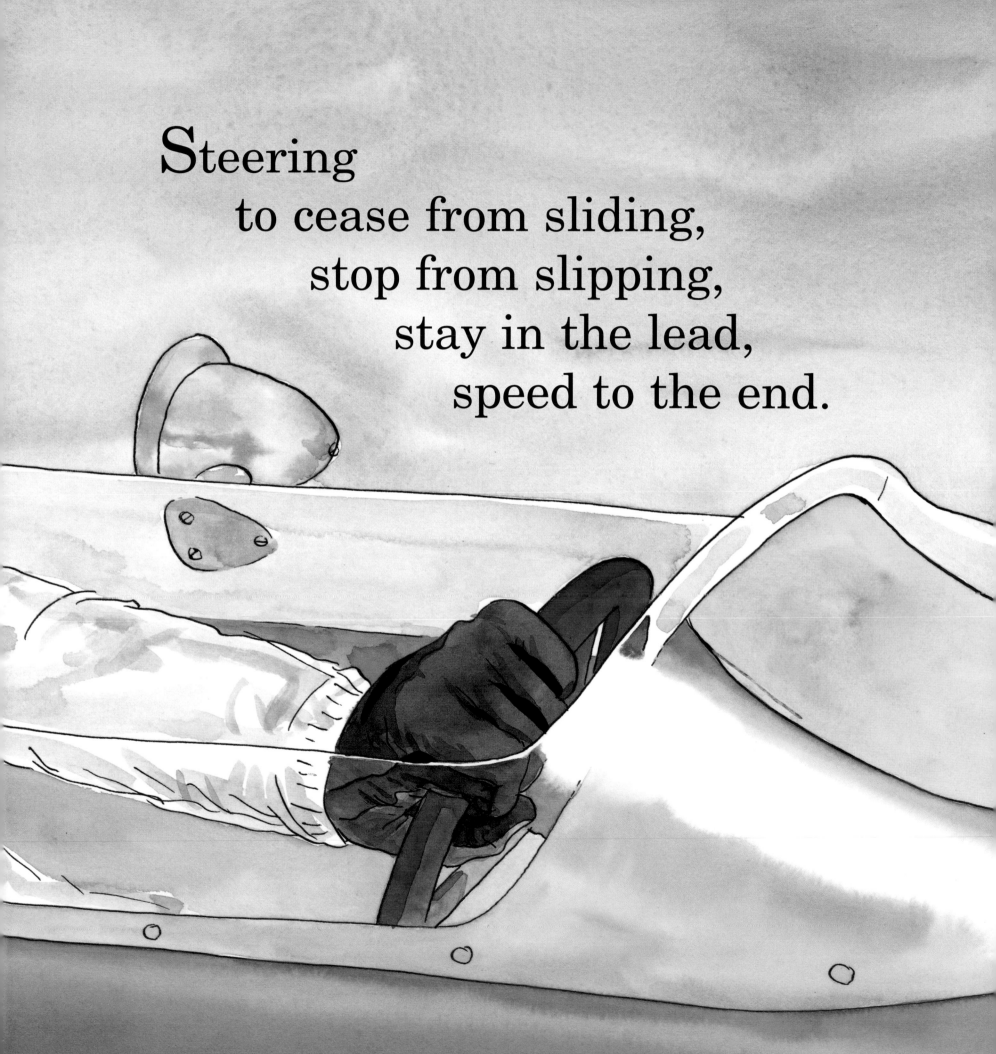

Steering
to cease from sliding,
stop from slipping,
stay in the lead,
speed to the end.

Tires
turning treads
taking cars
across the track.

Upended,
upset,
and
undone.

*Vroom*—
driver versus driver
veering, vying,
vowing victory.

Wheels—
when worn or wet—
wobble willy-nilly,
lead to weaving,
whacking walls.

# X-ray
## after an accident.

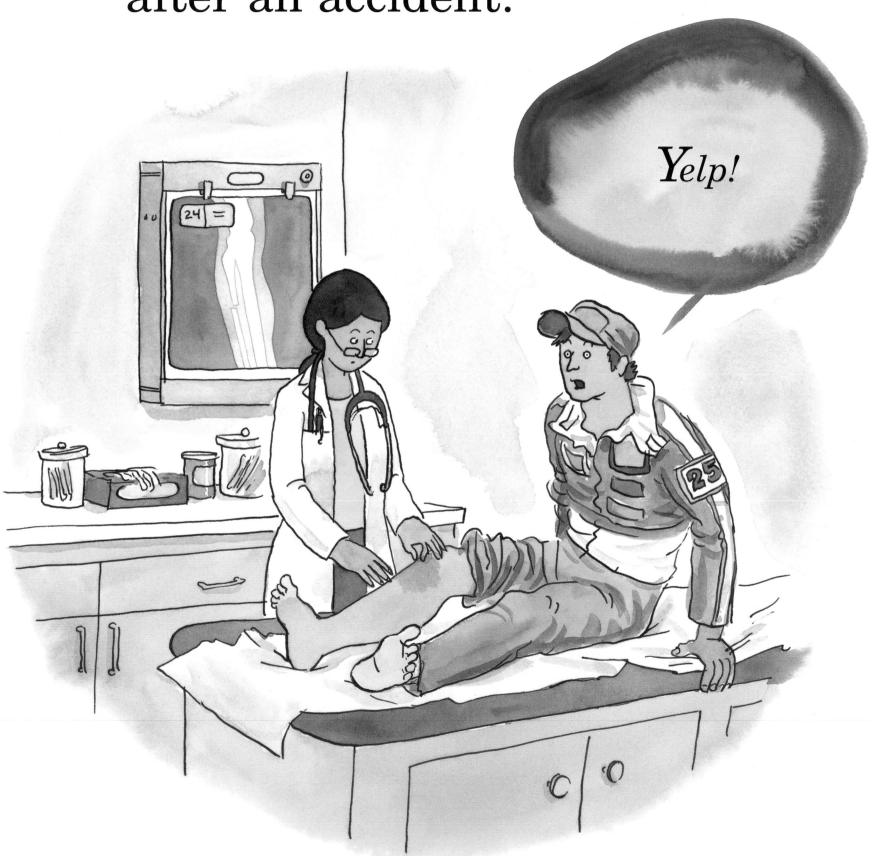